# THE SHAKESPEARE STORIES

ANDREW MATTHEWS
& TONY ROSS

4 BOOKS IN ONE!

Silver Dolphin
San Diego, California

**Silver Dolphin Books**
An imprint of Printers Row Publishing Group
10350 Barnes Canyon Road, Suite 100, San Diego, CA 92121
www.silverdolphinbooks.com

This text was first published in Great Britain in 2001 by The Watts Publishing Group

Text © Andrew Matthews, 2001
Illustrations © Tony Ross, 2002

Printers Row Publishing Group is a division of Readerlink Distribution Services, LLC.
Silver Dolphin Books is a registered trademark of Readerlink Distribution Services, LLC.

All notations of errors or omissions should be addressed to Silver Dolphin Books, Editorial Department,
at the above address. All other correspondence (author inquiries, permissions) concerning
the content of this book should be addressed to Orchard Books, Carmelite House,
50 Victoria Embankment, London EC4Y 0DZ, UK.

ISBN: 978-1-68412-163-2

Manufactured, printed, and assembled in Crawfordsville, IN, USA. LSC/03/17.

21 20 19 18 17 1 2 3 4 5

# contents

# Who Was William Shakespeare?

William Shakespeare was an English poet and playwright whose treasured works have been performed throughout the world and translated into most languages. Although much is known about his writings, Shakespeare himself remains a bit of a mystery.

Records suggest he was baptized on April 26, 1564, so his birthdate would have been a few days prior. Shakespeare grew up 100 miles northwest of London in a town called Stratford-upon-Avon. His father, John, was a leatherworker, and his mother, Mary Arden, was from a prominent local family. Shakespeare attended the local grammar school that would have included Latin and Greek curriculum, which would have exposed him to classic plays. In November 1582, at the age of 18, Shakespeare married Anne Hathaway, the daughter of a local farmer. They had three children, Susanna and twins Hamnet and Judith.

Shakespeare's life revolved around two locations: Stratford-upon-Avon and London. In London, he had a successful career as an actor, writer, and part owner of the company Lord Chamberlain's Men. In 1599, Shakespeare and Lord Chamberlain's Men built the Globe Theatre where they performed plays. In the years 1590-1613, Shakespeare wrote his most well-known works. Early plays were comedies and histories, and he wrote mostly tragedies until 1608 including *Hamlet*, *King Lear*, and *Macbeth*.

On April 23, 1616, William Shakespeare died in Stratford-upon-Avon. Over 400 years later, his works are celebrated around the world through festivals, read by students, and analyzed and reinterpreted by scholars. Shakespeare's plays are the most performed in the world, and their commentary on human emotion and conflict has transcended time.

# the Globe Theatre

Some of Shakespeare's most famous plays were first performed at the Globe Theatre, which was built on the South Bank of the River Thames in 1599.

Going to the Globe was a different experience from going to the theater today. The building was roughly circular in shape, but with flat sides. Because the Globe was an open-air theater, plays were put on only during daylight hours in spring and summer. People paid one English penny to stand in the central space and watch a play, and this part of the audience became known as the groundlings because they stood on the ground. A place in the tiers of seating beneath the thatched roof, where there was a slightly better view and less chance of being rained on, cost extra.

The Elizabethans did not bathe very often, and the audiences at the Globe were smelly. Fine ladies and gentlemen in the more expensive seats sniffed perfume and bags of sweetly scented herbs to cover the stink rising from the groundlings.

There were no actresses on the stage; all the female characters in Shakespeare's plays were performed by boys wearing wigs and makeup. Audiences were not well-behaved. People clapped and cheered when their favorite actors came on stage; bad actors were jeered at and sometimes pelted with whatever came to hand. Most Londoners worked hard to make a living and in their precious free time they liked to be entertained. Shakespeare understood the magic of the theater so well that today, almost four hundred years after his death, his plays still cast a spell over the thousands of people that go to see them.

✳  ✳  ✳

# Henry V

A shakespeare story

*For Marc*
*A. M.*

*For Kate and Jason*
*T. R.*

RETOLD BY ANDREW MATTHEWS
ILLUSTRATED BY TONY ROSS

# cast List

KiNg HeNry V

DUKe of EXeter
Uncle to the king

EARl of cambridge
A conspirator against the
king

Michael Williams

A soldier in the king's army

A French ambassador

A French messenger

The Scene

England and France in the fifteenth

century

*I see you stand like greyhounds in the slips,*
*Straining upon the start. The game's afoot.*
*Follow your spirit, and upon this charge*
*Cry, "God for Harry, England and Saint George!"*

King Henry; III.i.

Henry V

Hardly anyone called the new king
"Henry." When they talked about him
they said "Hal" or "Harry," or used one
of his other nicknames. Everyone knew
what a wild and rebellious teenager the
young prince had been.

Harry had spent more time with rascally old Sir John Falstaff learning how to drink and gamble  than he had with his royal father. Now the reckless young Harry was king, but no one knew what sort of king he would be. Some thought

 he would be a disaster; others said that only time would tell. But all were aware that the young king faced a difficult time as the new English monarch.

England and France had been at war for twenty-five years, and though the two countries had agreed to a truce, the truce was an uneasy one. A weak English king who didn't have the support of his people might give the French just the chance they wanted to carry out a successful invasion ...

✷ ✷ ✷

One morning, not long after Henry's coronation, the nobles of the high council were gathered together in the reception chamber of the king's palace in London. Among them was the Duke of Exeter, the king's uncle. He knew that Henry was now about to face his most challenging

test. "How young and lonely he looks on that great throne," Exeter thought. "He has his mother's dark hair and soft eyes—but does he have any of his father's courage, I wonder?"

His question was soon answered, for just then the doors of the great chamber opened and an ambassador from the dauphin, the crown prince of France, entered. The ambassador was a perfumed dandy with his curled beard, and the clothes he wore were as brightly colored as a peacock's feathers. Behind him, two guards carried a large wooden chest that they set down on the floor.

The ambassador gave an elaborate bow. "Your Highness," he said, in a voice as smooth as honey. "My master, the dauphin, sends greetings."

"I want more than greetings," Henry replied coldly. "I asked King Charles to give me back the French lands that my father won from him. What is his answer?"

The ambassador ran his fingers through the curls of his beard and smirked. "The king is busy with important matters," he said. "His Majesty thought that since the dauphin is closer to you in age, it would be better for him to deal with your request."

Henry felt a sting of anger at the ambassador's insolent tone, but he kept his voice calm. "And what is the dauphin's message?" he asked.

"The dauphin thinks you are a little too young to bother yourself with affairs of state," said the ambassador, gesturing toward the wooden chest. "So he has sent a present that he thinks will be more suitable than the right to French dukedoms."

The ambassador clicked his fingers,
and the guards opened the lid of the
chest. It was filled with tennis balls. One
of them fell out and rolled to the foot of
Henry's throne.

The nobles glanced at each other anxiously. King Henry had been insulted and humiliated in front of all his courtiers. How would he respond?

Henry leaned over and picked up the ball at his feet. He bounced it once and caught it in his right hand. "Tell the dauphin that he has begun a game with me that he'll wish he had never started,"  he said. "His mockery will turn these tennis balls into cannonballs! The people of France may be laughing at the dauphin's joke, but they'll weep before I'm finished!"

The ambassador's face went deathly pale. He bowed low and left the chamber. When the door closed behind him, the nobles began  to talk among themselves. Most of them glanced admiringly at Henry, but the Earl of Cambridge scowled at the king. He raised his voice above the hubbub in the chamber and said, "Your Majesty spoke hastily. You should have sought the advice of older and wiser men before plunging our country into war."

"An insult to me is an insult to the English people!" Henry snapped. "And besides, my lord Cambridge, I don't listen to the advice of traitors!"

Cambridge started as though someone had jabbed him with a knife point, and his eyes bulged with fear.

"You thought that because of my youth, I could easily be deceived," Henry went on, "but I've found you out. You betrayed your country for French gold and worked as a spy for King Charles. Guards, take him to the tower!"

The nobles stared in astonishment at
the disclosure of Cambridge's treachery
and at seeing the determination of their
young king. He was wiser and stronger-
minded than any of them had realized.

Men from all over the country answered the young king's call to war with France.

Blacksmiths,

farmworkers,

wheelwrights, weavers, and clerks . . .

. . . all left their homes and marched along
the roads that led to Southampton.

The younger men thought that war would be a kind of holiday and were eager for fame and glory; others, who had fought before and knew what battle was like, were grim-faced and silent.

At Southampton, the men began their
training. Hour after hour and day after
day they marched and drilled. At the
archery targets, men with longbows
practiced until their aim was true.

Slowly, the raggle-taggle band of
volunteers was transformed into an
army. When all was ready, the English
battle fleet set sail for the French port
of Harfleur.

***

It took all day for Henry's men to cross the Channel and unload the ships. The men spent the night on the beach and were woken in the gray hours before

dawn to sharpen their weapons and make
ready their siege ladders and battering
rams. On the skyline, the walls of
Harfleur looked like an ominous cloud.

When the sun rose, Henry rode out in front of his men on his dapple-gray warhorse, the early morning light glinting on his armor. "The English are a peaceful nation," he told the troops, "but when war comes, we can fight like tigers! Let the light of battle blaze in your eyes to burn the courage of your enemies! Let your cry be: *God for Harry, England and Saint George*!"

As the English army charged, cannons
roared like a gigantic wave breaking on
the shore. By nightfall, Harfleur had fallen.

\* \* \*

Henry was planning to advance to the port of Calais, which was already in English possession. The next morning, a messenger arrived from King Charles.

"The king commands that you surrender to him and leave France while you still can!" the messenger declared scornfully. "He is camped at Agincourt with an army of fifty thousand. If you do not agree to his terms, he will advance and crush you!"

"Your Majesty!" the Duke of Exeter murmured. "We only have four thousand men. If the French attack us here, all will be lost!"

"Then we must go to them, uncle," Henry said calmly. He turned to the messenger. "Tell King Charles that his army is in my way," he said. "I will march to Agincourt and if he does not step aside, the earth will be red with French blood!"

* * *

And so the English advanced to Agincourt
and set up camp facing the French on
a plain between two woods. When the
French saw the size of the English army
they whistled and jeered, beating their
swords against their shields to make a
great clamor.

But Henry shut his ears to their taunts and concentrated on positioning his forces. He  discussed battle plans with his commanders late into the night. After they left his tent, Henry tried to rest, but a whirlpool of doubts and fears swirled in his mind, and he could not sleep. Hoping to calm himself, he put on a hooded cloak and went walking through the camp.

Men lay asleep, huddled around fires. The air was filled with the sound of snores or voices shouting out in terror from nightmares. Across the plain glimmered the fires of the French camp, as numberless as the stars on a winter's night.

Henry was so deep in thought that he didn't notice a sentry on guard beside one campfire until he almost walked into the point of the man's spear.

"Who goes there?" barked the sentry.

"A friend," Henry replied.

"Who is your commander?"

"The Duke of Exeter."

The guard lowered his spear and pulled a face. "A fine soldier!" he grunted. "If he were leading the army instead of the king, we wouldn't be in this mess. I bet young Harry wishes he was back in London, tucked up safe in bed."

"The king wishes himself nowhere but here," said Henry.

The guard turned his head to spit into the fire. Light from the flames played across his broken nose and the long scar on his left cheek.

"Kings!" he growled. "They do the arguing, but it's the likes of you and me who do the fighting and the dying!"

"Tomorrow the king will fight in the front line alongside his men, you will see," said Henry.

"I'll wager a week's wages that he'll be at the back, with a fast horse ready for his escape!" the guard said bitterly.

"Very well," said Henry. "If we both survive, find me when the battle's over and we'll see who was right. What's your name?"

"Michael Williams," said the guard. "What's yours?"

"Harry le Roy," Henry said with a smile, then he passed on and disappeared into the darkness.

\*\*\*

In the early hours of the morning a thunderstorm broke. Rain fell mercilessly, drenching English and French alike and turning the plain into a sea of mud. The rain stopped just before dawn, but the sky was still filled with heavy black clouds.

The first line
of the French
army took
the field led
by knights on
horseback.
The plumes
on their helmets
fluttered brightly
against the dark sky, and their armor
shone like silver. Behind them
ran infantrymen in chain mail
coats carrying blue
shields painted with
golden fleurs-de-lis.

Henry ordered
his archers to stand
ready and wait for
his signal.

The French knights broke into a gallop. The hooves of the horses shook the ground and spattered their riders with mud. The knights lowered their lances and screamed out a battle cry, but halfway to the English line, the French horses

ran into boggy ground and the charge
faltered. The knights pulled at their reins
in panic, turning their horses to try and
find firmer footing. The infantrymen
caught up, and all was a surging chaos of
whinnying horses and cursing men.

Henry drew his
sword and swept
it high above his
head. "Fire!"
he bellowed.

At his command,
a thousand arrows
left a thousand
longbows and made
a sound like the wind sighing through the
boughs of a forest. A deadly hail struck the

French, piercing armor
and flesh and bone.
Knights fell from
their saddles and
startled horses
bolted, trampling
anyone who stood
in their way.

Volley after volley of arrows whistled down until the only movement on the battlefield came from the wounded as they attempted to crawl back to safety.

A second line of French troops charged.
Once more the English archers stopped
them. The French tried to retreat but ran

into their own third line as it came up
behind them. It was then that Henry led
his men in a charge. The two armies met
with a clash like a clap of thunder.

The fighting
lasted for two
hours. The
French soldiers,
dismayed
and confused,
found that their
commanders had
been killed and there

was no one to give them orders. They
fought bravely, but
the fury of
the English
attack
proved
too much
for them,
and at last
they broke
ranks and fled.

Seven thousand Frenchmen died at Agincourt, including many great noblemen. The English lost only a hundred men.

* * *

That night at sunset, a French messenger
rode into the English camp carrying a
white flag of truce. It was the same man
who had come to Harfleur, but this time
he was not haughty. His armor was dented
and there was dirt and blood on his face.

"King Charles begs for peace," he said humbly. "He will return all the lands that you claim, and he asks you to accept the hand of his daughter, Princess Catherine, so that your two families may be united in peace forever."

"Tell the king that I accept," said Henry. "We will meet and draw up a peace treaty."

That night, there were celebrations in
the English camp and just before midnight,
Henry slipped away from his commanders
and went in search of Michael Williams.
He found him at the same guard point as
on the previous night.

When Williams saw Henry, he dropped to one knee. "Your Majesty," he mumbled. "I did not know who you were last night, but I recognized you today when you led the charge."

"So," said Henry, smiling. "I won the wager."

"I was a fool to speak the way I did last night!" said the sentry apologetically.

Henry put his hand on the man's
shoulder and took a bag of gold coins
from his belt. He handed it to the
astonished guard.

"Here," Henry said. "You spoke your
mind last night. I hope that honest men will
always speak to me as openly as you did."

So King Henry the Fifth won a famous victory—and more importantly, he won the hearts of all his subjects. Now they respected him as a ruler, but they also loved him because he understood the lives of ordinary people and was always ready to listen to them.

And he won more than his subjects' hearts, for when he met Catherine, the French princess, they fell in love at once—even though she could not speak English and his clumsy French made her laugh. With their marriage, the bitter war with France was ended in feasting and friendship.

*And then to Calais; and to England then:*
*Where ne'er from France arrived*
*more happy men.*

King Henry; IV.viii.

# Patriotism in Henry V

There were no newspapers, radios, or televisions in Shakespeare's time, so it is difficult to know what ordinary people thought about what was happening in the world around them. However, dramatists often reflected popular opinions in their plays, and *Henry V* is an example of this.

Shakespeare wrote the play in 1599. The play is based on historical events, but Shakespeare shapes the facts to present a picture of a country uniting under a strong leader to face a fearsome enemy. The rousing patriotic speeches in the play capture the patriotic mood of Elizabethan England.

In *Henry V*, no one expects Henry to be a good king because of his wild behavior as a prince.

But once on the throne, he displays wisdom and courage.

On the night before the battle of Agincourt, Henry, disguised as an ordinary foot soldier, has a conversation with a sentry. Shakespeare presents a leader who is not distant from his people. This is a king in touch with his subjects, and one who values their honesty.

In the battle that follows, huge numbers of the French army are killed, while only a few Englishmen lose their lives. The audience, cheering the actors at the end of the performance, were expressing their patriotism and pride in their country and its achievements.

# A Midsummer Night's Dream

A Shakespeare Story

*To Hannah, love you more than . . .*
*A. M.*

*For Laura K.*
*T. R.*

RETOLD BY ANDREW MATTHEWS
ILLUSTRATED BY TONY ROSS

# Cast List

**Hermia**

In love with Lysander

**Helena**

Friend to Hermia
In love with
Demetrius

**Demetrius**

Betrothed to Hermia

**Lysander**

In love with Hermia

### oberon

King of the fairies

### ritania

Queen of the fairies

### puck

An elf

### Bottom

A weaver

## The scene

In and around Athens, ancient Greece

*Ay me, for aught that I could ever read,*
*Could ever hear by tale or history,*
*The course of true love never did run smooth.*

Lysander; I.i.

# A Midsummer Night's Dream

When the path of true love runs smoothly, the world seems a wonderful place—all bright skies and smiling faces.

Unfortunately, true love has a habit of wandering off the path and getting lost, and when that happens, people's lives get lost too, in a tangle of misery.

Take the love of Duke Theseus of Athens and Hippolyta, Queen of the Amazons, for instance. They were to be married, and their happiness spread through the whole of Athens. People had decorated their houses with flowers and left lamps burning in their windows at night so that the streets twinkled like a city of stars. Everybody was joyful and excited as they prepared to celebrate the duke's wedding day. Well, almost everybody . . .

\* \* \*

On the day before the royal wedding, two
friends met by chance in the market square:
golden-haired Hermia, and black-haired
Helena, both beautiful and both with secrets
that made their hearts ache.

For a while, the two friends chatted about nothing in particular. Then Helena noticed a look in Hermia's deep blue eyes that made her ask, "Is everything all right, Hermia?"

Hermia looked so sad and serious.

"I am to marry Demetrius tomorrow," she replied.

"Demetrius!" said Helena softly. Now her heart was aching worse than ever. Night after night she had cried herself to sleep, whispering Demetrius's name, knowing that her love for him was hopeless.

Many years ago the families of Hermia and Demetrius had agreed that, when they were of age, their daughter and son should marry. "You must be the happiest young woman in Athens!" sighed Helena.

"I've never been so miserable in my life!" Hermia declared. "You see, I don't love Demetrius."

"You don't?" cried Helena, amazed.

"I'm in love with Lysander," Hermia confessed, and she began to describe all the things that made Lysander so wonderful.

Helena thought about Lysander, with his curly brown hair and broad smile. He was *quite* handsome, she supposed, but he didn't have Demetrius's dark, brooding good looks. Why on earth did Hermia find him so attractive?

"Of course, I told my father that I didn't wish to marry Demetrius," Hermia said, "and he went straight to him to explain—but you know how stubborn Demetrius can be. He lost his temper and said it didn't matter who I loved, our marriage had been arranged and it must go ahead, no matter what. His stupid pride's been hurt, that's all—he doesn't love me a bit."

"Then who does he love?" Helena inquired eagerly.

"No one, except for himself," said Hermia. "I *can't* marry someone I don't love, and I know it will cause a scandal, but Lysander and I are going to run away together!"

"*When*?" Helena asked.

"Tonight," Hermia told her. "I'm meeting him at midnight in the woods outside the city walls. We plan to travel through the night, and in the morning we'll find a little temple where we can be married. Oh, Helena, it will be so *romantic*! Please say that you're happy for me!"

"Of course I am," said Helena. "I'm overjoyed."

And she was overjoyed—for herself. "At last, this is my chance!" she thought.

"If I visit Demetrius tonight and tell him that Hermia and Lysander have gone off together, he'll forget about his pride . . . and then . . . when I tell him how I feel about  him, he'll be so flattered, he'll fall in love with me. Love always finds a way!"

Which is true, but love doesn't always find the way that people expect, as Helena was about to find out. For it was not only in the human world that love was causing unhappiness; although Helena and Hermia did not know it, two different worlds would meet in the woods outside Athens that night, and the result would be chaos.

✳ ✳ ✳

Oberon, king of
the fairies, was
a creature of
darkness and
shadows, while his
wife, Queen Titania,
was moonlight and
silver. The two loved each

other dearly, but they had quarreled
bitterly. Titania had taken
a little orphan boy as a
page and made such
a fuss of the lad
that Oberon
had become
very jealous.
He wanted
the page
for himself.

That midsummer's night, in a clearing in the woods, Titania was singing to her page while fairy servants fluttered around her like glittering moths.

When Oberon appeared, Titania's silvery eyes darkened. "Fairies, let us leave this place at once!" she said haughtily.

"Wait, Titania!" snapped Oberon. "This quarrel of ours has gone on long enough. You say I have no reason to be jealous of the boy—very well, prove it! Give him to me!"

"Not for all your fairy kingdom!"
hissed Titania. She raised her left hand
and sent a ball of blue fire roaring across
the glade, straight at Oberon's head.

Oberon spoke a word of magic, and the fire turned to water that burst over him, drenching his clothes. By the time he had rubbed the water from his eyes, the glade was empty and Oberon was alone. "I'll make you sorry for this, Titania!" he vowed. Then, lifting his dripping head, he called out, "Puck? Come to me, now!"

A breeze sighed in the branches as an elf dropped out of the air and landed at Oberon's feet. The elf was dressed in leaves that had been sewn together. His hair was tangled, his skin as brown as chestnuts, and when he smiled, his white teeth flashed mischievously. "Command me, master!" Puck said.

"I mean to teach the queen a lesson," said Oberon. "Go, search the earth and fetch me the flower called love in idleness."

"I will fly faster than a falling star!" said Puck, and with that he vanished.

A cruel smile played on Oberon's lips. "When Titania is asleep, I will drop the juice of the flower in her eyes," he said to himself. "Its magic will make her fall in love with the first living thing she sees when she wakes—perhaps a toad or even a spider! She will make herself seem so ridiculous, that she will beg me to break the spell, and I will . . . after she's given me the page!"

This plan pleased Oberon so much that he began to laugh—but his laugh was cut short when he heard human voices approaching. With a wave of his fingers, Oberon made himself vanish among the shadows.

✳ ✳ ✳

Demetrius, out searching for Hermia, halted in the middle of the glade while he considered which path to take. This gave Helena a chance to catch up with him. "Wait for me, Demetrius!" she pleaded.

Demetrius scowled at her. "For the last time, Helena, go home!" he shouted angrily. "I can find Lysander and Hermia without your help."

"But you don't understand!" Helena exclaimed. "I love you! I've always loved you!"

She tried to put her arms around Demetrius, but he ducked away. "Well, I don't love you!" he said roughly. "So go away and leave me alone!"

And he ran off through the moonlight.

"Oh, Demetrius!" sobbed Helena, running after him. "I would follow you through fire, just to be near you!"

✳ ✳ ✳

When the glade was once more still and silent, Oberon came out of the darkness. His face was thoughtful. "I must help that lovely maiden!" he whispered. "I know how cruel it is to love someone whose heart is so cold."

A wind brushed the fairy king's cheek, and there stood Puck, holding a sprig of glimmering white flowers.

"Take two blossoms and search the

woods for a young human couple,"
Oberon said to him. "Squeeze the juice of
the petals into the young man's eyes, but
do it when you are sure that the maiden
will be the first thing he sees."

"At once, master!" Puck said with a

bow, and then he was gone.

Then Oberon went to find Titania.

He found her sleeping alone on a bank of violets, and the air was heavy with their sweet perfume. As he dropped juice from the magic flowers onto Titania's eyelids, Oberon murmured:

*"What you see when you awake,
Do it for your true love take!"*

＊ ＊ ＊

At that very moment, in another part of
the woods, Puck was putting magic juice
into the eyes of a young man he had
found sleeping next to a young woman at
the foot of a pine tree.

"When he wakes and sees her, his love
for her will drive him mad!" Puck giggled,
and he leapt into the air like a grasshopper
in a summer meadow.

But, as bad luck would have it, Puck
had found the wrong couple. Those
sleeping under the tree were Lysander and
Hermia, who had got lost in the woods
and exhausted themselves trying to find
the way out.

And as bad luck would also have it, a
few seconds after Puck had
left them, Helena
wandered by,
searching for
Demetrius.
Blinded by tears,
Helena did not
notice Lysander
and Hermia
until she
stumbled over
Lysander's legs.

He woke, saw her and
his eyes bulged like a
frog's as the magic
went to work.

"Lysander?"
gasped Helena.
"What are you
doing here? I mean,
you mustn't be here! Get away quickly!
Demetrius is looking for you, and if he
finds you . . ." Her voice
trailed off—there was
a strange look about
Lysander, and it
made her feel
uncomfortable.
"Why are you
staring at me like
that?" she asked.

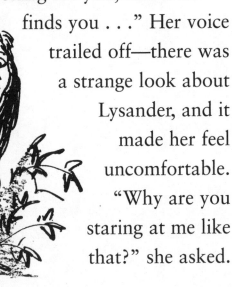

"Because at last I have found my own true love," said Lysander. "Helena, can't you see how much I love you?"

Helena stepped back, laughing nervously. "Don't be silly, Lysander!" she said. "You love Hermia . . . don't you?"

"Hermia, who is she?" scoffed Lysander, scrambling to his feet. "How could I love anyone but you, with your eyes like stars, your hair as black as ravens' wings and your skin as soft as . . ."

"That's quite enough of that!" said Helena. "This is some sort of midsummer madness!"

"Madness? Yes, I'm mad!" said Lysander. "Mad with love for you! Come to my arms and cool the fires of my passion with your kisses!"

He moved toward Helena, but she turned and fled. Lysander followed her shouting, "There's no escape from love, Helena! This was meant to be!"

Their loud voices and pounding footsteps woke Hermia. "Lysander, where are you?" she muttered sleepily. "Don't wander off on your own, my love. You might be eaten by a lion, or a bear . . ." The very thought made her wide awake, and she sat up. "Or I might be eaten, come to that!" she said with a shudder. "I'm coming to find you, Lysander, so we can be eaten together!"

* * *

Not five paces from the bank of violets where Titania lay asleep, a group of Athenians had gathered in secret to rehearse a play that they meant to perform for duke Theseus after his wedding. One of the actors, a weaver called Bottom, was behind a tree, waiting to appear when he heard his cue. "I'll show them how it's done!" Bottom said to himself. "When the duke sees what a fine actor I am, he'll give me a purse of gold, or my name's not Nick Bottom!"

He glanced up and saw a strange orange light circling the tree. "Now what's that, I wonder?" he muttered. "A firefly perhaps?"

It was Puck. He had noticed the actors as he flew by on his way back to Oberon and had seen a chance to make mischief. "Behold, the queen's new love!" he said. Magic sparks showered down from his fingertips onto the weaver.

Immediately Bottom's face began
to sprout hair, and his nose and ears
grew longer and longer. His body was
unchanged, so Bottom had no idea that
anything was wrong, until he heard his
cue and stepped out from behind a tree.

Bottom had meant his entrance to be
dramatic, and it certainly was. The other
actors took one look at the donkey-
headed monster coming toward them
and raced away screaming and shouting.

"What's the matter with them?" said Bottom, scratching his chin. "My word, my beard has grown quickly today! I'll need a good shave before the performance tomorrow!" He paced this way and that, puzzling out why his friends had left in such a hurry. "O-o-h! I see-haw, hee-haw!" he said at last. "They're trying to frighten me by leaving me alone in the woods in the dark! Well, it won't work! It takes more than that to frighten a man like me-haw, hee-haw!"

And to prove how brave he was, Bottom began to sing. His voice was part human, part donkey and it sounded like the squealing of rusty hinges. It woke Queen Titania from her sleep on the bank of violets. "Do I hear an angel singing?" she said, and raised herself on one elbow and gazed at Bottom. "Adorable human, I have fallen wildly in love with you!" she told him.

"Really?" said Bottom, not the least alarmed by the sudden appearance of the fairy queen. He was sure it was all part of the trick his friends were playing.

"Sit beside me so I can stroke your long, silky ears!" Titania purred. "My servants will bring you anything you desire."

"I wouldn't say no to some supper," said Bottom. "Nothing fancy—a bale of hay or a bag of oats would suit me fine!"

From up above came the sound of Puck's laughter, like the pealing of tiny bells.

Oberon's laughter set every owl in the woods hooting. "My proud queen, in love with a donkey?" he cried. "Well done, Puck! Titania will think twice before she defies me again! But what of the humans?"

"I did as you commanded, master," said
Puck. "I found them . . ."

A voice made him turn his head, and he
saw Demetrius stamping along the path,
dragging Hermia by the arm.

"That is the fellow!" said Oberon. "But
who is that with him?"

"He is not the one I cast the spell on!"
Puck yelped.

"Quickly," said Oberon. "Make yourself
invisible before they see us!"

✳ ✳ ✳

Hermia was thoroughly miserable.
Everything had gone wrong: she had
found Demetrius instead of Lysander,
and Demetrius was in such a foul temper
that she feared the worst. "Oh, where is
Lysander?" she wailed. "You've killed
him, haven't you, you brute?"

With a weary groan, Demetrius let Hermia go and slumped to the ground. "I haven't touched your precious Lysander!" he yawned. "Now stop whining and get some sleep. When it's light, we'll find our way out of these accursed woods."

"I won't rest until I find Lysander!" Hermia said defiantly.

"Just as you wish," said Demetrius. "I'm too tired to argue anymore."

He lay back among the ferns and closed his eyes. He heard Hermia walking away, and then he fell into a deep sleep.

Moonlight shifted and shivered as Oberon and Puck reappeared. "This is the man," said Oberon, peering down at Demetrius. "Search the woods for a black-haired maiden and bring her here. When she is close by I will put magic juice in his eyes and wake him."

"Yes, master! But tell me, is human love always so complicated?" Puck asked curiously.

"Just do as I have commanded!" snapped Oberon.

Helena was still running with Lysander just a few steps behind her. So many bewildering things had happened to her that when an orange light appeared above the path in front of her, she was not surprised—in fact, a curious idea suddenly popped into her mind—Puck's magic had put it there. Helena became convinced that if she followed the light, it would lead her

114

back to Athens, and sanity. Over streams and through clearings the light led her, until at last she came to a deep thicket of ferns, where she paused for breath.

"Helena, marry me!" she heard Lysander shout.

"I don't want you!" she shouted back. "I want Demetrius!"

"And here I am, my love!" said Demetrius, springing up out of the ferns nearby, his eyes glowing with magic. "Hold me, let me melt in your sweetness!"

Helena did not bother to wonder why Demetrius had changed his mind: her dreams had come true, and she was about to rush into his arms when Lysander ran between them. "Keep away from her, Demetrius!" Lysander said hotly. "Helena is mine!"

"Lysander . . . is that you?" called a voice, and Hermia came stumbling out of the bushes. Brambles had torn the hem of her dress, and there were leaves and twigs stuck in her hair. "Thank the gods you're safe!" she said, weeping for joy. "Why did you leave me, my only love?"

"Because I can't bear the sight of you!" said Lysander. "I want to marry Helena."

"So do I!" Demetrius exclaimed. "And since she can't marry both of us, we'll have to settle the matter, man to man!"

He pushed Lysander's chest, knocking him backward, then Lysander pushed Demetrius.

Hermia stared at Helena, her eyes blazing. "You witch! You've stolen my Lysander!" she screeched.

"I haven't stolen anybody!" Helena replied angrily. "This is all some cruel trick, isn't it? The three of you plotted together to make a fool of me —and I thought you were my friend!"

"Our friendship ended when you took Lysander away from me!" snarled Hermia.

And there might have been a serious
fight if Oberon had not cast a sleeping
spell on all four of them. They dropped to
the ground like ripe apples, Hermia falling
close to Lysander and Helena collapsing at
Demetrius's side.

Oberon and
Puck appeared
magically
beside them.
"Smear their eyes
with fairy juice!"
said Oberon. "This knot
of lovers will unravel when they wake."

As Puck hurried about his task, the air
was filled with the singing of fairy voices.
"The queen!" Puck muttered in alarm.
"The queen is coming!"

✳ ✳ ✳

Titania did not notice Puck and Oberon, or
the sleeping lovers. She could see nothing
but Bottom, whose jaws were stretched
open in a wide yawn. "Are you weary,
dearest one?" she asked him tenderly. "Rest
with me on these soft ferns."

"I feel a powerful sleep coming over me-haw, hee-haw!" said Bottom.

"Fairies, leave us!" ordered Titania.

The fairies flew away, leaving bright trails in the air. Titania cradled Bottom's head in her lap, and they both dozed.

Oberon and Puck crept close. Puck began to grin, but he stopped when he saw the sorrow in his master's eyes.

"There is no laughter in this!" Oberon sighed. "How I long for Titania to smile at me as she smiled at this creature, and to feel her soft arms around me as I sleep! Break the spell on the human, Puck, while I deal with the queen."

Oberon moved his hands, weaving
shadows into magic as he chanted:

*"Be the way you used to be,*
*See the way you used to see,*
*Wake, my queen, and come to me!"*

Titania opened her eyes, and when she
saw Oberon she flew into his arms. "I am
so glad that you are here, my love!" she
said. "I had the strangest dream! I dreamed
that I had fallen in love with a . . ."

"We will never quarrel again," Oberon promised. "Keep your page—have fifty pages if you wish! What does it matter, as long as we are together."

Puck saw that the sky was getting lighter. "It's almost dawn, master!" he warned.

"Then we must leave!" said Oberon, and he, Titania and Puck faded into the pale morning light.

* * *

When the sun rose, its light woke
Demetrius and Helena, who fell in love
at first sight, then Lysander and Hermia,
who fell in love all over again. There was
much smiling, sighing and kissing, and
soon Demetrius said, "Today is Duke
Theseus's wedding day, as well as mine

and Helena's. Come, my friends, the priest
can marry us all at the same ceremony!"

And the lovers hurried off toward
Athens, laughing every step of the way,

the paths of their true love running smoothly at last.

✳ ✳ ✳

And as for Bottom, he woke sometime later and clambered stiffly to his feet. "I thought I was . . . !" He mumbled. "I

thought I had . . . !" Anxiously, he felt his face and ears and then sighed with relief.

"What a midsummer night's dream!" he exclaimed. "I'll write a poem about it and read it to Duke Theseus and his bride, and the duke will say: 'Well done, noble Bottom! Here's some gold for you!'"

And he stumbled away through the

ferns, making up lines of poetry and reciting them out loud as he went.

*The eye of man hath not heard, the ear of man hath not seen, man's hand is not able to taste, his tongue to conceive, nor his heart to report what my dream was.*

Bottom; IV.i.

# Love and Magic in

## A Midsummer Night's Dream

In *A Midsummer Night's Dream,* Shakespeare brings together two worlds: the human world of Athens, and the fairy world of the woods outside the city. One world is ruled by law, the other by magic, and in both worlds trouble is brewing.

In the woods outside Athens, Oberon and Titania are busy arguing over a page boy. Meanwhile Demetrius, who is as stubborn as Oberon, is insisting on marrying Hermia, even though she loves someone else. Add a group of bickering actors and Puck, a mischievous sprite, and madness follows.

The humans are made to love the wrong partners, and Titania falls in love with one of the actors, who has the head of a donkey!

When the human lovers begin to fight one another, the play comes close to tragedy, but magic sets things right. The humans find their true loves and Oberon realizes that his love for Titania is stronger than his pride.

The Elizabethans believed in a "midsummer madness" that was caused by the heat of the summer sun, and many of the characters in *A Midsummer Night's Dream* behave as if they have been touched by this madness.

The fairy world and the human world are thrown into chaos by love, and Shakespeare pokes fun at how lovers behave. And in the character of Bottom he makes fun of actors—and even playwrights like himself too!

# The Merchant of Venice

A Shakespeare story

*For May, with love*
*A. M.*

RETOLD BY ANDREW MATTHEWS
ILLUSTRATED BY TONY ROSS

# cast List

**Antonio**

A Venetian merchant

**Bassanio**

Antonio's young friend,
in love with Portia

**Portia**

A noblewoman of Belmont,
in love with Bassanio

**Nerissa**

Portia's maid

shylock

A Venetian moneylender

The Prince of Arragon

Portia's suitor

The Prince of Morocco

Portia's suitor

The Duke of Venice

Judge at Antonio's trial

The Scene

Venice in the sixteenth century

*I will buy with you, sell with you,*
*walk with you, and so following;*
*but I will not eat with you, drink with you,*
*nor pray with you.*


Shylock; I.iii.

# The Merchant of Venice

One afternoon in the city of Venice, two men stood together on a bridge over a canal. The older man, Antonio, was a successful merchant. His companion was his friend Bassanio. Antonio had just told Bassanio a scandalous piece of gossip, but Bassanio did not seem interested.

"What's wrong, Bassanio?" said Antonio. "You've hardly spoken a word to me."

Bassanio peered down at the canal. "Last year, I visited the town of Belmont. I had dinner there with a man who had a beautiful daughter named Portia," he said.

She was wise, witty—"

"And you fell in love with her?" interrupted Antonio.

Bassanio blushed. "I've been thinking about her ever since," he confessed. "Two days ago, I learned that Portia's father has died, leaving her all his fortune. She is one of the richest women in Italy."

Antonio slapped his friend on the back. "Then go to Belmont and woo her!" he urged.

"Rich suitors are flocking to propose to Portia—even princes from foreign lands!" groaned Bassanio. "What chance would I stand against them? I can't even afford a new suit of clothes!"

"How much money do you need to woo Portia in style?" Antonio asked.

"Three thousand ducats," replied Bassanio.

Antonio lowered his voice so that passersby would not hear him. "If I had the money, I would lend it to you," he said. "But at the moment, I haven't got three hundred ducats, let alone three thousand. All my money is invested in four ships that are voyaging around the world. When they return to Venice, I'll be a wealthy man again, but until then . . ."

"So you can't help me?" Bassanio cried in despair.

"My reputation is still good," said Antonio. "Find a moneylender who will loan you three thousand ducats, and I will sign a bond promising to repay him."

Bassanio beamed. "You are the best friend a man could have!" he declared.

✳ ✳ ✳

While Bassanio and Antonio were talking on the bridge in Venice, in Belmont the lovely Portia paced to and fro across a richly furnished room. Her serving maid, Nerissa, watched from a chair in the corner. In the center of the room was an oak table, and on it were three caskets—one made of gold, another of silver, and the third made of lead.

Suddenly, Portia stopped pacing and stamped her foot. "This is so unfair!" she grumbled. "I'm an intelligent, educated woman, but can I choose a husband for myself? Oh no! The man who marries me must select one of these stupid caskets. If he picks the right one, I have to be his wife."

"That was one of the conditions of your father's will, Miss," said Nerissa. "If you hadn't agreed to it, you wouldn't have inherited his money." A far-off look came into Nerissa's eyes. "I know who I'd pick as a husband for you," she said.

"Who?" demanded Portia.

"That Venetian gentleman who came to dinner last summer," Nerissa cooed.

A faint redness crept into Portia's cheeks. "His name was Bassanio, wasn't it?" she said.

"So it was!" exclaimed Nerissa. "There was something special about him, and if you ask me, he thought you were special too, Miss."

Portia's cheeks turned a deeper red. "Nonsense!" she said. "Bassanio has probably forgotten all about me!"

As the sun set over Venice, Bassanio strolled around a public square discussing business with Shylock the moneylender, who was a thin man with a long grizzled beard.

Shylock had a sharp mind but often pretended to be slow-witted to mislead his clients. He frowned at Bassanio and said, "Let me be clear about this. You want to borrow three thousand ducats?"

"I do," said Bassanio.

"And your friend, the merchant Antonio, will sign a bond guaranteeing that he will pay back the money within three months?"

Bassanio nodded. "He will," he said.

"Look, here comes Antonio now. He'll tell you himself."

Shylock narrowed his eyes. He and Antonio detested each other, though both

men made a show of being polite.

"Well, Shylock!" said Antonio. "Will you lend Bassanio the money?"

"I am considering it," Shylock replied. "It surprises me that you're willing to sign a bond. Didn't I hear you boast that you would never charge interest on a loan or pay interest on any money that you borrowed?"

"Normally, I wouldn't," agreed Antonio. "But this money is for my friend, so I'm making an exception. Will you give him the money or not?"

Shylock spoke quietly but sparks of rage glowed in his eyes. "Antonio, you have

often criticized the way I do business, but I have never complained," he said. "The other day, you spat on my clothes, called me a dog and kicked me. Today, you're asking for my help.

Remember that I am just as human as you. If you cut me, I bleed, if you poison me, I die—and if you insult me, I will have my revenge."

"We don't like each other, Shylock," Antonio said frankly. "If I don't return your loan in time, imagine the pleasure it will give you to make me pay the penalty."

Shylock laughed as if he had thought of a joke. "Speaking of the penalty, I think it would be amusing if the lawyer who draws up the bond writes that if you do not pay me by such and such a date, you will let me cut off a pound of your flesh from the place nearest your heart. Agree to that, and your friend shall have his money," he said.

Bassanio clutched Antonio's arm. "No, Antonio!" he gasped. "Let's find another moneylender."

Antonio sensed that Shylock was testing him. If he refused Shylock's terms, the moneylender would spread the word that Antonio was a coward.

"Just as you wish, Shylock," Antonio said.

"No!" said Bassanio. "What if something happens to your ships?"

"Don't worry!" Antonio said. "They are due back in Venice a month before the repayment date."

Neither Antonio nor Bassanio noticed Shylock's gloating smile.

"Sailors make mistakes, and ships sink, Antonio!" Shylock thought. "Once that bond is signed, you will be at my mercy!"

In Belmont, Portia led the Prince of Morocco into the room where the caskets were kept. The prince was a handsome man, whose white robes showed off his dark skin. He stared at the caskets, picked up the one made of lead and read the words inscribed on it. *"If you choose me, you must risk all that you have."*

The prince put
down the casket.
"Risk all that
I have—for
lead?" he snorted.
"I will risk
nothing for a
common metal.
What is the inscription
on the silver casket? *If you
choose me, you will get as much as you
deserve.*" The prince
laughed. "This
could be the right
casket. I deserve
the best, and
Lady Portia
would be the
best wife for me.

But I'll wait until I've read the inscription on the gold casket. *If you choose me, you will get what many men desire.* This must be the one! Many men want to marry Lady Portia, and a prize like her must be in a casket made from the most precious metal of all!"

The prince lifted the lid of the gold casket and cried out in dismay. Inside was a human skull with a small roll of parchment in one of its eye sockets.

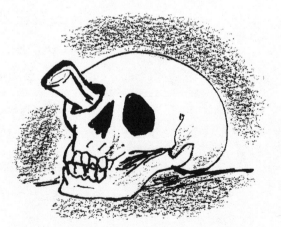

The prince unrolled the parchment, and read:

*All that glistens is not gold,*
*As you often have been told.*
*You have chosen outward show,*
*So now say farewell, and go.*

Without another word, the prince
left the room, and Portia heaved a sigh
of relief.

The next afternoon in Belmont,
the Prince of Aragon took his turn at
choosing between Portia's three caskets.
He stroked his beard and spoke his
thoughts aloud. "Lead is too crude for my
taste," he said, "and gold is too obvious.
I choose the silver casket."

The prince opened the casket and found a miniature painting of a man dressed as a jester. With the painting was a parchment scroll, which read:

*This picture makes it plain to see*
*That you have chosen foolishly.*
*Though you are strong, your mind is weak*
*And you are not the one I seek.*

The prince bowed to Portia. "I will not make an even bigger fool of myself by staying any longer, my lady," he said, and left.

The next moment, Nerissa burst into the room. "You'll never guess who I met in town, Miss!" she jabbered. "Bassanio! He's on his way here to ask you to marry him. Isn't it romantic?"

Portia felt as excited as Nerissa but kept her feelings hidden. "Romantic or not, he will have to take the test like all the other suitors," she said solemnly.

Bassanio and Portia were delighted to meet again. Portia explained the peculiar conditions of her father's will. Bassanio admitted that he was poor and described how and why Antonio had borrowed money from Shylock.

Finally, Bassanio said, "Show me the caskets. Let me choose."

Portia was afraid. If Bassanio chose wrongly, she would lose him forever.

"Wait a few days!" she begged.

"I can't bear to," said Bassanio. "I have to know if we're to spend our lives together or apart."

Portia led Bassanio to the room where the caskets were kept, and he examined them. "Evil often disguises itself," he said. "In court, a guilty man hides his crime behind a clever argument. Cowardly soldiers mask their fear by pretending to be brave. But this lead casket doesn't seem to be hiding anything."

With shaking hands, Bassanio opened the casket. Inside was a portrait of Portia and a scroll that read:

*You have not chosen with your eyes,*
*But with your heart, and you are wise.*
*Turn now to where your lady is,*
*And claim her with a loving kiss.*

So, Bassanio and Portia were married and were blissfully happy. As the weeks turned into months, Bassanio almost forgot about his previous life. Then one morning at breakfast, he received a letter from Venice. As he read the letter, he gasped in horror.

"Is it bad news?" inquired Portia.

"The worst!" Bassanio said. "Antonio's ships have been lost at sea. Shylock has had him thrown into prison and says that Antonio must keep his bond."

"Give Shylock his three thousand ducats!" exclaimed Portia. "Give him six thousand if he wants."

"Shylock's daughter ran off and got married. She took money from her father's cash boxes. The shock has hardened Shylock's heart," Bassanio said. "He insists on his pound of flesh. Antonio goes on trial for debt in a few days."

"We owe him our happiness," said Portia. "You must go and see him at once."

While Bassanio was packing for his trip, Portia called Nerissa to her and told her about Antonio.

"Poor fellow!" Nerissa sighed.

"I'm going to help him!" announced Portia. "My cousin, Dr. Bellario, taught me a lot about the law when I first tried to understand father's will. I'll call on him, ask him for a letter of introduction to the Duke of Venice, and discuss Antonio's case. Then you and I are are off to Venice—disguised as lawyers!"

On the day of Antonio's trial, all Venice seemed to be packed into the courtroom. The Duke of Venice sat in the judge's chair with Shylock to his left and Antonio and Bassanio to his right.

The Duke signaled for silence and said,

"Where is the lawyer Balthazar, sent by
Dr. Bellario to defend Antonio?"

Portia and Nerissa stood up and bowed.
They were wearing lawyers' robes, and
Portia had glued on a false beard. "Here
I am, my lord!" she said in a deep voice.

"You may begin!" declared the duke.

Portia turned to Shylock. "Will you give up the bond if Antonio returns the three thousand ducats he borrowed from you?" she asked.

"I would not give it up for sixty thousand ducats!" Shylock hissed.

"Antonio," Portia said, "were you tricked into signing the bond?"

"No," replied Antonio.

Portia shrugged. "Then the bond is legal, but Shylock must be merciful," she said.

"Merciful?" hooted Shylock. "Why must I be merciful?"

"Because mercy brings a blessing both to those who receive it, and those who give it," Portia told him.

"I don't want to be blessed!" grunted Shylock. "I want justice to be done!"

"Show me the bond!" said Portia.

The clerk of the court handed her a parchment, which she read quickly. "The moneylender is right," she said. "The law is on his side. Antonio, unfasten your shirt and prepare to die."

"Give me your hand, Bassanio," whispered Antonio. "Good-bye, my friend!"

Shylock produced a dagger and began to sharpen it on a small stone.

"Take care when you cut, Shylock," Portia advised.

"Why?" snapped Shylock.

"According to the bond, you can cut off a pound of Antonio's flesh from the place closest to his heart, but there is no

mention of blood," Portia said. "Shed one drop of his blood, and the state of Venice will confiscate everything you own."

Shylock knew that he had been outwitted. He glowered at Portia.

"Give me my three thousand ducats!" he snarled.

"You have already refused the money in open court," Portia pointed out.

The duke spoke severely to Shylock. "According to the laws of Venice," he said, "if someone plots to take another's life, half his property will be confiscated by the state, and the other half will be given to his intended victim."

Shylock's face went pale. "I have lost everything!" he whimpered. "You may as well sentence me to death!"

"Will you show Shylock any mercy, Antonio?" said Portia.

Antonio looked at Shylock and saw not a loathed enemy, but a broken old man. "I wish to end the hatred between us," he said. "Let Shylock keep my half of his property."

The duke stood up. "The case is closed," he said. "All are free to go."

The crowd in the courtroom cheered and chanted Antonio's name.

Bassanio forced his way through the throng and caught Portia by the arm. "Master Balthazar, you have saved my best friend's life!" he gushed. "I swear that I will give you anything you ask for."

Portia smiled.
"Then I will
have your gold
ring," she said.

Bassanio's
face fell. "That is
my wedding ring!"
he said. "I swore to my
wife that I would always keep it safe."

"And you swore to me
that you would give
me anything
I asked for," said
Portia. "Your
wife is married
to a man who
thinks nothing
of breaking
promises."

Reluctantly, Bassanio removed the ring and presented it to Portia. "When she learns how much I owe you, my

wife will understand why I gave you my wedding ring."

"Oh, I know she will!" Portia assured him.

Then she and Nerissa slipped away and left Venice to its celebrations.

*The quality of mercy is not strain'd*
*It droppeth as the gentle rain from heaven*
*Upon the place beneath: it is twice blest;*
*It blesseth him that gives, and him that takes.*

Portia; IV.i.

# Love, Hate and Mercy in The Merchant of Venice

The story closest to the plot of *The Merchant of Venice* appeared in a collection of stories by the Italian writer Ser Giovanni, which was published in Milan in 1558. Shakespeare probably used it as the basis of his play, which he wrote sometime between 1596 and 1597. Though *The Merchant of Venice* comes very close to tragedy, it is classed as a comedy because of its happy ending.

Shylock is a villain because greed and hatred have twisted his personality. He considers Antonio a fool for not charging interest on the money that he lends.

Antonio has good qualities—he is a loyal and generous friend—but his treatment of Shylock is shameful, and it is easy to understand why Shylock wants to be revenged on him. The merchant is also rash, or he would never have agreed to Shylock's outrageous terms. Another mark of his rashness is how willing he is to risk all he has on the voyages of four ships.

In contrast to this dark tale of hatred and prejudice is the love story of Portia and Bassanio. Like Antonio, Portia is bound by the law—in her case, the terms of her father's will. She is beautiful and highly intelligent. The Prince of Morocco and the Prince of Arragon are not worthy of her. They choose the gold and silver caskets because they cannot see beyond outward appearances. It is the impoverished Bassanio who makes the right choice and allows true love to win.

Without Antonio's help, Portia and Bassanio would never have married, and that is why Portia decides to disguise herself as a lawyer and travel to Venice to defend Antonio in court.

# Hamlet

A shakespeare story

*For Mum*
*A. M.*

*For Guy and Philippa*
*T. R.*

RETOLD BY ANDREW MATTHEWS
ILLUSTRATED BY TONY ROSS

# cast List

The ghost of Hamlet's father

## Hamlet

Son to the former king
Nephew to Claudius

## Gertrude

Queen of Denmark
Mother to Hamlet

## Horatio

Friend to Hamlet

## Claudius

King of Denmark

## Laertes

Son to Polonius

## ophelia

Daughter to Polonius

## Polonius

Lord Chamberlain

A troop of traveling players

## The scene

Denmark in the thirteenth century

*Murder most foul, as in the best it is,*
*But this most foul, strange, and unnatural.*

Ghost of Hamlet's father; I.v.

# Hamlet

Snowflakes twirled in the wind that moaned around the battlements. I turned up the collar of my cloak against the cold and kept my eyes fixed on the place where the guards had told me they had seen my father's ghost.

Horatio, my oldest friend, was with me. It was Horatio who had brought me the news that my father, the king, was dead— bitten by a snake while he was sleeping in the orchard—and it was Horatio who had stood by my side at my father's funeral. Something in me died too that day and was sealed up in the royal tomb with my father. My grief was so great that it sucked the light and joy out of everything.

From the courtyard below came the sound of drunken laughter.

"Someone is still celebrating the marriage of your mother and your uncle!" Horatio said.

He meant it as a joke, but the joke raised more black thoughts in my mind.

"How could she marry so soon after the funeral?" I said. "How could she forget my father so quickly?"

"You should be happy for her, my lord Hamlet," said Horatio. "She has found new happiness in the midst of sorrow, and your uncle, Claudius, will rule Denmark wisely until you come of age."

I laughed bitterly. I had seen cunning in Claudius's face, but no wisdom. I was about to say so, when midnight began to ring out from the turret above our heads.

And as the last stroke throbbed through the air, the darkness and the falling snow shaped themselves into the spirit of my father beckoning to me.

Horatio gasped out a warning, but I paid no attention. I ran through the dancing flakes, my heart beating so fast that I thought it would burst. The ghost was dressed in armor, a circlet of gold gleaming against the black iron of its helm. Its face was my father's face but twisted in agony, its eyes burning like cold, blue flames. Its voice was a groan of despair that sent shudders down my backbone.

"Hamlet, my son! My spirit cannot find rest until my murder has been avenged."

"Murder?" I cried.

"The serpent who stung me in the orchard was my brother, Claudius," said the ghost. "As I lay asleep, it was he who crept to my side and poured poison in my ear. Claudius took my life, my throne and now my wife. Avenge me, Hamlet!"

Before I could say more, the ghost faded into snowy blackness, and the echoes of its voice became the whistling of the wind.

My mind reeled. Had I really spoken to the ghost of my father, or was it a devil from hell sent to trick me into doing evil? I had suspected that Claudius might have had something to do with my father's death, but could I trust the word of a vision from beyond the grave? How could I be sure of the truth? How could I, the prince of Denmark, not yet twenty years old, avenge the death of a king?

I turned and stumbled back to Horatio. His face was gray and he quivered with fear. "Such sights are enough to drive a man mad!" he whispered.

I laughed then, long and hard, because Horatio had unwittingly provided me with an answer.

Who could have more freedom than a mad prince? If I pretended to be mad, I could say whatever I wished and search for the truth without arousing Claudius's suspicion.

And so my plan took shape. I wore nothing but black. I wandered through the castle, weeping and sighing, seeking out shadowy places to brood. If anyone spoke to me, I answered with the first wild nonsense that came into my head, and all the time I watched Claudius, looking for the slightest sign of guilt. I cut myself off from all friends—except Horatio; I told him everything, for I knew he was the only one I could trust.

A rumor began to spread through the castle that grief had turned my wits. So far my plan was a success, but it is one thing to invent a plan, and another thing to carry it through. The strain of pretending, of cutting myself off from kindness and good company, was almost too great to bear. There were times when I thought I truly had gone mad, when I felt I could no longer carry the burden of what the ghost had told me. If I avenged my father, my mother's new husband would be revealed as a murderer, and her happiness would be shattered; if I did not, my father's soul was doomed to eternal torment.

Worst of all, I was tortured by doubt.
What if Claudius were innocent? What if I
had been deceived by an evil spirit?
Questions went spinning through my mind,
like the stars spinning around the earth.

Then one day, on a bleak afternoon,
alone in my room, I drew my dagger and

stared at it. The blade
was sharp: if I used
it on myself, death
would come
quickly, and all
my doubts and
worries would be
over—but what
then? Would I
be sending my
soul into an even
worse torture?

I weighed the dagger in my hand, balancing the fear of what I must do to avenge my father against the fear of what might follow death. It seemed I lacked both the courage to go on with my life and the courage to end it.

Hearing a knock at my door, I sheathed the dagger and called out, "Come in!" almost relieved at the interruption.

A woman entered. It was Lady Ophelia, her fair hair shining like a candle flame, her eyes filled with love and concern.

My heart lifted, then sank. Ophelia and I had loved each other since we were children. Before my father's death, I had been certain that she was the one I would marry—but now everything had changed. There was no room in my heart for love.

"Lord Hamlet?"
Ophelia said.
"My father asks
if you will attend
the performance
of the Royal
Players tonight?"

As soon as she mentioned her father,
I knew what was happening. Her father
was Polonius, the royal chamberlain, a
meddling fool who loved gossip and secrets.
He had sent Ophelia to try and discover
why I was acting so strangely. Ophelia
would report everything I said to Polonius,
and he would report it to Claudius. I was
sickened: the castle of Elsinore was a place
where brothers murdered brothers, wives
forgot their husbands and fathers used their
daughters as spies.

I laughed carelessly to hide the ache I felt when I looked at Ophelia's beautiful face. "Tell Lord Polonius that I shall be at the play," I said.

Ophelia turned her head, and I saw a tear fall across her cheek. "My lord," she murmured, "why do you never look at me the way you used to? There was a time when I believed you loved me and wished us to marry, but now you seem so cold . . ."

I longed to tell her how much I loved her and that my coldness was nothing more than acting, but I did not dare. "*You* marry me?" I said roughly. "Marry no one, Ophelia! Wives and husbands are all cheats and liars. It would be better for you to join a convent and become a nun!"

At this she ran from the room, her sobs echoing through the corridor, making my heart break.

And then, just as I thought there was no end to my despair, an idea came—first a glimmer, then a gleam then a burst of light brighter than the sun.

I hurried from my room and went to the great hall, where the actors were setting up their stage. I found their leader, a tall man with a look of my uncle about him. After chatting for a few moments, I said casually, "Do you know the play *The Murder of Gonzago*?" "Certainly, my lord!" came the reply.

I handed the man a purse filled with gold. "Act it tonight," I said. "But I want you to make some changes to the story. Listen carefully . . ."

I meant to turn the play from an entertainment into a trap—a trap to catch a king.

That evening, while the audience watched the stage, I watched Claudius. At first he showed little interest in the story, preferring to whisper to my mother and kiss her fingers in a way that filled me with loathing—but gradually the skill of the players won his attention.

At the end of the first scene, exactly according to my instructions, the actor playing Duke Gonzago lay down as though asleep, and his nephew Lucianus—played by the actor who resembled Claudius—crept up on him and poured poison into his ear.

Even though the light in the hall was dim, I could see the deathly pallor of Claudius's face as he watched this scene. His eyes grew troubled, and he raised a trembling hand toward the stage.

I knew then that I was gazing at the face of a murderer and that everything the ghost had told me was true.

"No!" Claudius cried out, springing to his feet. "Lights! Bring more lights!"

But all the torches in the world would not light the darkness in his mind. His nerve failed and he hurried from the hall.

Mother started to follow him, but I stopped her at the door. "Do not delay me. I must go to the king!" she said. "Something is wrong."

"And I know what," I told her. "I must talk to you. I will come to your room in an hour. Make sure you are alone, and tell no one of our meeting."

But I underestimated Claudius's cunning and the power he had over my mother. When she let me into her room, there was a coldness in her expression and I guessed that she had been speaking to my uncle. Before I could say a word, she said, "Hamlet, you have deeply offended your royal stepfather."

"And you have offended my dead father," I replied.

Mother frowned at me, puzzled. "What do you mean?" she demanded.

"You offended him the day you abandoned your mourning robes in exchange for a wedding gown," I said. "The day you married a liar and a murderer!"

"I won't listen!" Mother shouted. She began to cover her ears with her hands, and I caught hold of her wrists to prevent her—she had to hear the truth. Mother screamed in alarm, and then I heard a voice from behind the drawn curtains at her window, calling out, "Help! Murder!"

I was certain it was Claudius—who else would skulk and spy in my mother's bedroom? I drew my sword and plunged it into the curtain. Fierce joy overcame me that my father was avenged at last . . .

But it was the body of Lord Polonius
that tumbled into the room; I had killed
an innocent man.

"You meddling old fool!" I groaned.
"What were you doing there?"

"Following my orders," said a voice.

I turned and saw Claudius in the doorway
with two armed guards. A triumphant light
glinted in his eyes. "I was afraid you might
harm your mother if you were alone with
her," Claudius went on.

"Your madness has made you violent,
Hamlet. You must leave Denmark tonight.
I shall send you to friends in England
who will care for you until you are back
in your right mind. Guards, take the
prince away!"

Neither my mother nor the guards saw the mocking smile that flickered on his lips, but as soon as I saw it, I knew that Claudius intended me never to return from England. I would be imprisoned, and then secretly murdered.

While I had been trying to trap my
uncle, he had been setting a trap for me,
and now it had snapped shut.

They bundled me into a windowless
carriage and locked the doors and I
was driven speedily through the night.

I could see nothing and could hear only
the rattling of the wheels and the cracking
of the driver's whip, keeping the horses at
full gallop.

After several hours, the carriage arrived at a port, and I was placed on a ship that set sail almost as soon as I was aboard. I made no attempt to escape. It was all over: my father was unavenged, Claudius had outwitted me and I was as good as dead.

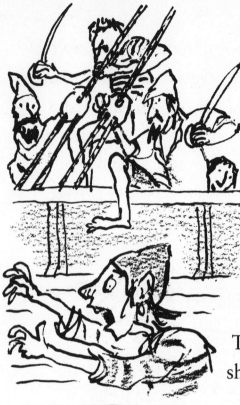

Just before dawn broke, my life seemed to become some strange dream, for the most unlikely thing happened: I was rescued by Danish pirates. They captured the ship and murdered most of the crew, but when they discovered who I was, panic seized them. Fearing that they would be hunted down by the Danish fleet, the pirates sailed back to Denmark and put me ashore at a little fishing village.

There I found lodgings and wrote letters to Horatio and to my mother. I told her that I would return to Elsinore and right all the wrongs that had been done— though I did not tell her what those wrongs were.

The next day, I bought a horse and set

off, certain that Fate had returned me to Denmark to complete my revenge. There was no more doubt in my mind— Claudius was guilty, and I would make him answer for his crime.

I was still some way from the castle

when I was met by Horatio, who had ridden out to find me. There was a darkness in my friend's face, and I knew he was the bearer of ill tidings.

"My lord," he said, "the Lady Ophelia is dead. Claudius told her that you had killed her father, and the grief drove her so mad that she drowned herself."

Tears blurred my sight. What had I done to my beloved Ophelia! In another time and place our love might have grown into happiness . . .

"Ophelia's brother, Laertes, has sworn to kill you for the deaths of his father and sister," Horatio went on, "but Claudius persuaded Laertes to settle his differences with you in a fencing match in front of the whole court. I have seen the king whispering to Laertes in private, and I am sure they are plotting against you. Turn back, my lord! Escape while you can to someplace where you will be safe!"

"No, I must go to Elsinore," I told him. "My destiny awaits me there. We cannot escape our destinies, Horatio, we can only be ready for them, and I am ready."

\* \* \*

And so the ghost, Claudius, the pirates
and my destiny have brought me back to
the torchlight and candles of the great hall
at Elsinore. Courtiers and nobles chatter
idly and make wagers on the outcome of

the duel. There, on the royal thrones, sit
my uncle and my mother. She smiles at me
and looks proud; he is anxious and keeps
glancing slyly at Laertes. Laertes is filled
with a cold hatred that makes his eyes
shine like moonlight on ice.

Horatio takes
my cloak and
hands me a
rapier. His face is
pale and worried.
He leans close and
whispers, "Have a
care, my lord! There
is death in Laertes's look."

I smile: death is everywhere in the castle
of Elsinore tonight,
and I can feel my
father's spirit
hovering over me.
Claudius raises
his right arm.
"Let the contest
begin!" he
commands.

The blades of our rapiers click and squeal. Our shadows, made huge and menacing by the torches, flicker on the walls as we duck and dodge. Laertes is a skilled swordsman, but rage and hate have made him clumsy. He drops his guard to strike at me, I flick my wrist and the point of my rapier catches his arm.

One of the marshals shouts, "A hit! First hit to Prince Hamlet!"

Laertes bows, his forehead slick with sweat. "Let us take a cup of wine and catch our breath, my lord," he says.

The wine cups are on a table near the thrones. Laertes and I step toward them, and my mother suddenly snatches up one of the cups. "A toast to honor my beloved son!" she announces.

"No!" hisses Claudius. He reaches out as if to dash the cup from my mother's lips, but he is too late: she has drunk the wine down to the dregs.

There is just time for me to see a look of horror on Claudius's face, and then, without warning, Laertes wheels around and slashes at me with his sword. I parry the blow, realizing that this is no longer a contest—I am fighting for my life.

I see Laertes's eyes, blind with fury. I watch his mouth twist itself into an ugly snarl. He clutches at me and tries to stab under my arm, but I catch the sword in my left hand and I wrench it from his grasp. A pain like fire burns against my palm, and my fingers are wet with blood.

I step back, throw Laertes my rapier and take his in my right hand. "En garde!" I say.

We fight on, but something is wrong. Laertes looks terrified, and his breath comes in sobs. The pain in my hand is fierce, throbbing up into my forearm—I have suffered from sword cuts before, but none as painful as this.

Laertes lunges desperately at me, and the point of my sword scratches through his shirt; a spurt of red stains the whiteness of the linen.

Laertes reels back. "We are dead men!" he groans. "The king spread poison on the blade—the same poison that he poured into your wine cup!"

I see all now. I understand the hot agony that is creeping through my left arm and across my chest.

Laertes cries out, "The king is a murderer!" and crumples to the floor. At the same time, my mother screams and topples from her throne.

There is no
time left. I must
act quickly, before
the pain reaches
my heart. I stagger
toward Claudius,
and he cringes in
his throne,
covering his face
with his hands.

"Traitor!" I say,
and drive the poisoned
sword deep into his heart.

Voices shout . . . people are running. I
fall back, and someone catches me. I think
it is Horatio, but I cannot see him clearly,
for a darkness is falling before my
eyes . . . coming down like the snow
falling, that night on the battlements . . .

Through the darkness, I seem to see
a light . . . and my father's face . . . and
everything drops away behind me . . .

Horatio's voice whispers, "Farewell,
sweet prince!"

And the rest is silence.

*There's a divinity that shapes our ends,*
*Rough-hew them how we will.*

Hamlet; V.ii.

# Revenge in Hamlet

In *Hamlet*, Shakespeare portrays a young man who has been educated to be a thinker but who becomes a man of action, motivated by the dark force of revenge.

When Hamlet discovers from his father's ghost that the old king's death was not an accident but murder, he is torn in two. The ghost claims that the murderer is Claudius, his own brother, who has recently married Hamlet's mother. Is the ghost telling the truth, or is it a demon sent from hell to tempt the prince into an evil act? Hamlet is left confused and constantly tortured by doubt. He can't decide what to do.

In a desperate attempt to uncover the truth, Hamlet pretends to be mad. He kills Polonius by mistake, and this leads to the accidental death of

Ophelia, with whom Hamlet was once in love.

In a thrilling climax, Hamlet agrees to a fencing match with Laertes. Laertes, having lost his father and sister, is full of despair and desire for his own revenge. He fights with a poisoned sword given to him by Claudius, who suspects that Hamlet knows too much.

In Elizabethan times, this final scene of *Hamlet* was full of spectacularly gory visual effects. To make sword fights seem more realistic, pigs' bladders filled with blood were hidden in the actors' costumes and pierced with the point of a sword or dagger.

The audience was likely spellbound by the dark tale of revenge, where a prince succeeds in avenging his father's death—but at a terrible cost.

# shakespeare stories

RETOLD BY ANDREW MATTHEWS

ILLUSTRATED BY TONY ROSS

As You Like It

Hamlet

A Midsummer Night's Dream

Antony and Cleopatra

The Tempest

Richard III

Macbeth

Twelfth Night

Henry V

Romeo and Juliet

Much Ado About Nothing

Othello

Julius Caesar

King Lear

The Merchant of Venice

The Taming of the Shrew